CUMBRIA LIBRARIES

3 8003 04847 1106

KT-408-006

This book belongs to:

_ _ _ _ _ _ _

This paperback edition first published in 2018 by Andersen Press Ltd.
First published in Great Britain in 2017 by Andersen Press Ltd.,
20 Vauxhall Bridge Road, London SW1V 2SA.
Copyright © Tony Ross, 2017.
The right of Tony Ross to be identified as the author and
illustrator of this work has been asserted by him in accordance
with the Copyright, Designs and Patents Act, 1988.
All rights reserved.
Colour separated in Switzerland by Photolitho AG, Zürich.
Printed and bound in China.

1   3   5   7   9   10   8   6   4   2

British Library Cataloguing in Publication Data available.
ISBN 978 1 78344 588 2

OUR KID

Tony Ross

Andersen Press

Our Kid was late for school again.

He didn't have his homework or his uniform either,
so his teacher sent him straight to the Naughty Corner.

"Please, Sir," squeaked Our Kid.
"I left on time this morning
and my mum said,
'Remember to take
your homework.'

And my dad said, 'Go **straightly** to school, Our Kid. Don't be late **again**.'

So I **shoffled** my homework into my bag and took the **shortcut**.

When you take the shortcut
along the beach,
you have to dunkle your
hooves in the water.

Suddenly a submarine splooshed up out of the waves and squeaked across the sand.

Peeping in a porthole, I saw it was full of water.
And the water was full of fish.

Their leader, Captain Mackerel,
said that they were chasing pirates and
could take me to school on the way.

As it was too watery inside the submarine, I rode on
the deck, and off we bumpeeded down the road.
But before the fish could find the pirates...

... the pirates found the fish!
These were dinopirates, so some were
squiddly, but others were felumpingly big.

The big ones shook the
submarine.

The fish were safe inside, but I fell into the pirates' clutches.

They snitched my trousers and my schoolbag.

"My homework's in that!" I cried, as the pirates sniggled and bounded away.

I tried to **stop** them, but they were too big.
And if I had, they probably would've **eaten** me.

"Hello!"

boomdered a voice.

An elephant had snuck up behind me. He was not a wild elephant, because he was wearing a belt and a shed on his back.

He asked me, 'Why so glumbumtious, little goat?'

I told him how late I was for school, so he
offered me a lift, high up on his back.

Which was lucky, because it was a long way over the craggly mountains and across the wide blue water. And I got to see it all, without getting snarked by crocodiles.

When we got to school I said thank you
and the elephant kerlumped away.

And that's why I got here so late,
without my homework or my trousers."

"Our Kid, be hushled!" cried the teacher.

"Children, what do we call someone who makes up such total and utter nonsense?"

A good goat is on time, does their homework and never lies.

But just then...

Kerumble!

The school began to shake. Desks tipped over and chairs bounced around as everybody scrambled out of the nearest window or door.

But **Our Kid** wasn't allowed to leave the Naughty Corner... so he was still there when **three** aliens walked in!

"We were here to get a dinosaur," they said.

"Our museum only has an old one. The one we found had these shorts with your name inside."

The **dinopirate** was excited to be visiting a new planet and the whole class waved goodbye as the spaceship ʒerumbled off.

Then everyone ran back inside.

"You were bravey to face the aliens like that," said his teacher.

Our Kid handed in his homework and the teacher gave him a gold star and an apple, without even reading it.

"You can be as late as you like tomorrow," he chuckled.

This time Our Kid skipped straightly home,
with no shortcuts and his head full of adventures.

"You're back early," said his mum.
"So, what happened **today**?" asked his dad.

"Nuffin," said Our Kid.

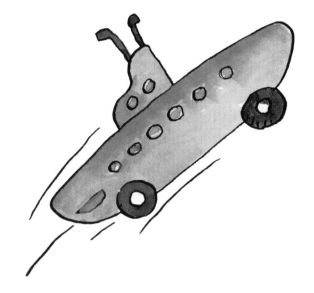